Sebastian Sasquatch

Sylvia Olsen

Illustrated by Kasia Charko

Library and Archives Canada Cataloguing in Publication

Olsen, Sylvia, 1955–
Sebastian Sasquatch / Sylvia Olsen ;
Kasia Charko, illustrator.

ISBN 978-1-55039-197-8

1. Sasquatch—Juvenile fiction.
I. Charko, Kasia, 1949– II. Title.

PS8579.L728S42 2012 JC813'.6 C2012-901958-5

Sono Nis Press most gratefully acknowledges support for our publishing program provided by the Government of Canada through the Canada Book Fund and the Canada Council for the Arts, and by the Province of British Columbia through the British Columbia Arts Council and the Book Publishing Tax Credit, Ministry of Provincial Revenue.

Edited by Laura Peetoom and Dawn Loewen
Proofread by Audrey McClellan
Cover and interior design by Frances Hunter

Published by
Sono Nis Press
Box 160
Winlaw, BC V0G 2J0
1-800-370-5228
books@sononis.com

Distributed in the U.S. by
Orca Book Publishers
Box 468
Custer, WA 98240-0468
1-800-210-5277

www.sononis.com

Printed and bound in Canada by Houghton Boston Printing.

Printed on acid-free paper that is forest friendly (100% post-consumer recycled paper) and has been processed chlorine free.

The Canada Council for the Arts | Le Conseil des Arts du Canada

ACKNOWLEDGEMENTS

This story started out as one I told, not one I wrote. Over the years, and after much telling, I received wonderful input from many people. I can't thank everyone, but here are the names of some of the people who made this story so much better than it would have been otherwise: Rita Morris and her 2010–11 Grade 2 class, and Janet Pistell and her 2010–11 Grade 4/5 class, at Lau'Wel'New Tribal School in Tsartlip, B.C.; Saralie Pincini, who heard the story in Toronto; Shelagh Kubish, Melanie Rousseau, Lesley Sutton, and Nikki Tate, who read the story and gave feedback; Laura Peetoom and Dawn Loewen, my astounding editors, who are full of good ideas. And can you imagine Sebastian any other way than how the talented Kasia Charko created him? Kasia is wonderful to work with. Thank you all, and thank you to Diane Morriss and Sono Nis Press for continuing to publish life-affirming stories.

To

Reuben, Silas, and Joey,

the little boys who inspire me

Sebastian Sasquatch lives in Puddle Valley. It is the most beautiful place in the world. Puddle Creek is surrounded by fields of lupines, buttercups, roses, and tiger lilies. The mountains around the valley are covered with giant Douglas-fir and cedar trees. Sebastian climbs high into the tall trees until the spindly tops bend over with his weight.

Sebastian loves Puddle Valley. He swings in the trees like a monkey from limb to limb with his very long arms. He swims in Volcano Lake until he is so cold his hair stands straight up. He fishes in Puddle Creek until his stomach is so full he can hardly climb back up the bank.

Sometimes Sebastian plays hide-and-seek with Brooklyn the bear cub. Brooklyn says she likes Sebastian because he has long, thick brown fur like hers. But even if Sebastian washes his long, soft fur so it shines in the sun, Brooklyn mostly prefers to play with other bear cubs.

Sometimes Sebastian plays tag with Ferdinand the fawn. Ferdinand says she likes to play with Sebastian because of his big smile. But no matter how much Sebastian smiles his friendliest smile, Ferdinand never wants to play for long.

Sebastian's father plays with him sometimes, but he is very busy doing grown-up things. Sebastian's mother plays with him once in a while, but she's also very busy doing grown-up things. Sebastian wishes there were just one sasquatch child in Puddle Valley to play with.

But even if Sebastian were to run all day and into the night, he would not find another sasquatch child. There are no sasquatch children for at least a few days of running, and that is too far to go to find a friend.

So most of the time Sebastian plays all by himself, carving little sasquatches in wood and stone, following animal tracks, and chasing butterflies and squirrels around Shooting Star Meadow. He plays until he is so tired he falls into a heap on the grass and goes to sleep.

TOOLS

PUDDLE VALLEY
CAMPGROUND
and
Adventure
Park

Very close to Sebastian's home is the Puddle Valley Campground and Adventure Park. It is a wonderful place, full of children. They arrive with their families in the spring and stay until late in the summer, and they are the closest things to sasquatch children Sebastian has ever seen. But they are not sasquatch children. Mother says they are human children, and that it is best to stay away from Puddle Valley Campground and Adventure Park.

"It is a place for humans. You have Shooting Star Meadow and Volcano Lake and all the rest of Puddle Valley to play in," says Mother. "Only very special human children can see sasquatches. I doubt you're going to find one at the Puddle Valley Campground and Adventure Park."

But Sebastian is lonely, so he sits outside the fence at the campground and watches human boys and girls laughing and playing. Even when Sebastian sits up tall and waves and smiles, no one looks his way.

"It's best that you play with your animal friends," Father says later. "Only very special human children want to play with sasquatches."

If only Sebastian could find a very special human child, then he would be able to play too.

One day Sebastian sees a little girl riding a shiny red bicycle. It has streamers floating from the handle grips and brightly coloured beads on the spokes that make a cheerful clicking sound when the wheels turn around.

Sebastian is sure this girl must be very special to have such a beautiful bicycle. So he leaps out from behind the fence and jumps up and down. He wiggles his ears. He smiles a very big smile. He dances his fanciest dance steps in front of the girl.

But the girl rides her bicycle right past him without even looking his way.

Late the next day Sebastian sees a girl with fluorescent pink running shoes. They are the finest-looking running shoes he has ever seen. They sparkle brightly like stars on a clear night—and that's not all. Each time the girl takes a step, lights flash on and off like tiny pink and silver flames.

Sebastian is sure she must be a very special girl to have such wonderful running shoes. So he leaps out from behind the fence and winks at the girl. He whistles his favourite tune and claps his hands. He stands on one hand and wiggles his toes. He curls into a perfect somersault, rolling up onto his feet as smoothly as a stream tumbling over river stones. He takes a bow: "Ta da!"

But the girl runs right past him as though he isn't even there.

The next day Sebastian sees a boy who stands head and shoulders taller than the other boys. This boy can run faster and jump higher than his friends. When they play baseball, the boy hits the ball farther than any of them. Sometimes he hits it so hard the ball sails over the fence and all the way into the woods.

Sebastian is sure the boy must be very special. So he leaps out from behind the fence and stands up tall. He flexes his muscles and struts proudly in front of the boy. "Look at me, look at me!" Sebastian says.
He stands on his hands and gracefully flips backwards, landing perfectly on both feet.

But the boy walks right past him without so much as a nod or a wink.

Sebastian slumps against a tree and stares at the sky. Surely he has found three very special children, but not one of them wants to play with him.

When Sebastian gets home he says, "Father, you told me that only very special human children want to play with sasquatches. Today I saw three special children, and they all walked by without even looking at me!"

Sebastian describes the little girl with the bicycle and the girl with the brightly coloured running shoes, how they sparkled and blinked. He tells his father about the boy who could hit the ball and how it sailed right over the fence and into the woods.

Sebastian's father says, "Oh, my son, special is not about running shoes or bicycles or hitting a ball. Special is something that is inside a human. Something that makes a person see what others don't."

The next day Sebastian sits on an old cedar log near the fence. He puts his elbows on his knees and his chin in his hands. He watches the children run back and forth laughing and calling to one another. If being special is something that is inside a human, how is he to know which child will want to play with him?

"I'm never going to find a human friend," Sebastian says to himself. "I don't even know what sort of child is special."

Not far from Sebastian sits a small boy under a tree. He doesn't have brightly coloured running shoes or a shiny new bicycle, and he isn't doing anything special—just whittling a smooth branch of yellow cedar.

Sebastian sighs loudly.

The small boy lifts his head and looks around.

Sebastian's furry eyebrows go up. He tries a little cough.

The small boy looks in Sebastian's direction.

Sebastian stands up. The boy stands up.
Sebastian stamps his feet. The boy stamps his feet.
Sebastian claps his hands. The boy claps his hands.
Sebastian laughs. The boy laughs.

Sebastian says, "I'm Sebastian. Do you want to play with me?"

The boy nods and smiles a big smile. He puts his whittling down on the log and says, "I'm Jack. Do you want to play with me?"

"Oh, yes, I do!" Sebastian says.

Pretty soon the two of them are standing on their heads and turning somersaults. They are running and jumping. Sebastian puts Jack on his shoulders and swings like a monkey with his long arms from limb to limb through the forest. They whittle a fine figure of a Douglas-fir tree. They whistle and sing and giggle until the day is late and Jack points toward his tent.

"I have to go home now," he says.

Sebastian suddenly worries. What if Jack won't play with him again? Is Jack really special? He seems so ordinary.

Jack can see Sebastian. He has even played with Sebastian. All Sebastian knows is that Jack has made him feel very special indeed. Perhaps that is the thing that makes Jack special.

Jack says, "I'll see you tomorrow!"

"Yes," says Sebastian, grinning. "And I will see you too!"